COMING SOON

Mr. Gum and the
Gingerbread Billionaire

Contents

You're a Bad Man,
Mr. Gum!

ANDY STANTON
Illustrated by CHAD DEZERN

HARPERCOLLINS*PUBLISHERS*

You're a Bad Man, Mr. Gum!

Text copyright © 2006 by Andy Stanton

Illustrations copyright © 2008 by Chad Dezern

www.harpercollinschildrens.com

Library of Congress Cataloging-in-Publication Data

Stanton, Andy.

You're a bad man, Mr. Gum! / Andy Stanton ; illustrated by Chad Dezern. — 1st American ed.

　　p.　cm.

Summary: Brave-hearted young Polly attempts to stop mean old Mr. Gum from poisoning Jake, a huge dog adopted by the town of Lamonic Bibber that keeps destroying Mr. Gum's garden, and thus provoking the angry fairy who lives there. Includes a glossary of such English terms as gob and trouserface.

ISBN 978-0-06-115240-5 (trade bdg.)

ISBN 978-0-06-115243-6 (lib. bdg.)

[1. Eccentrics and eccentricities—Fiction. 2. Dogs—Fiction. 3. Fairies—Fiction. 4. Courage—Fiction. 5. England—Fiction. 6. Humorous stories. 7. Fantasy.] I. Dezern, Chad, ill. II. Title. III. Title: You are a bad man, Mr. Gum!

PZ7.S793246You 2008	2007030701
[Fic]—dc22	CIP
	AC

1　3　5　7　9　10　8　6　4　2

❖

Text originally published in 2006 by
Egmont UK Limited, London
First U.S. Edition, 2008

1

The Garden of Mr. Gum

Mr. Gum was a fierce old man with a red beard and two bloodshot eyes that stared out at you like an octopus curled up in a bad cave. He was a complete horror who hated children, animals, fun, and corn on the cob. What he liked was snoozing in bed all day, being lonely, and scowling at things. He slept and scowled and picked his nose and ate it. Most of the towns-folk of Lamonic Bibber avoided him, and the children were terrified of him. Their mothers would say, "Go to bed when I tell you to or Mr. Gum will come and shout at your toys and leave slime on your books!" That usually did the trick.

Mr. Gum lived in a great big house in the middle of town. Actually, it wasn't that great, because he had turned it into a disgusting pigsty.

The rooms were filled with junk and pizza boxes. Empty milk bottles lay around like wounded soldiers in a war against milk, and there were old newspapers from years and years ago with headlines such as:

VIKINGS INVADE BRITAIN

and

WORLD'S FIRST NEWSPAPER INVENTED TODAY

Insects lived in the kitchen cup-boards—not just small insects, but great big ones with faces and names and jobs.

Mr. Gum's bedroom was absolutely grimsters. The wardrobe contained so much mold and old cheese that there was hardly any room for his moth-eaten clothes, and the bed was never made. (I don't mean that the duvet was never put back on the bed, I mean that the bed had never even been *made*. Mr. Gum hadn't gone to the bother of assembling it. He had just chucked all the bits of wood on

the floor and dumped a mattress on top.)
There was broken glass in the windows,
and the ancient carpet was the color of
unhappiness and smelled like a toilet.

Anyway, I could be here all day
going on about Mr. Gum's house, but I
think you've got the idea. Mr. Gum was
an absolute lazer who couldn't be bothered with niceness and tidying and
brushing his teeth, or anyone else's teeth
for that matter.

(and as you can see, it's a big "but") he
was always extremely careful to keep his
garden tidy. In fact, Mr. Gum kept his
garden so tidy that it was the prettiest,
greeniest, floweriest, gardeniest garden

in the whole of Lamonic Bibber. Here's how amazing it was:

> Think of a number between 1 and 10.
> Multiply that number by 5.
> Add on 350.
> Take away 11.
> Throw all those numbers away.
> Now think of an amazing garden.

Whatever number you started with, you should now be thinking of an amazing garden. And that's how amazing Mr. Gum's garden was. In spring it was bursting with crocuses and daffodils. In summer there were roses, sunflowers, and those little blue ones—what are they called again? You know, those blue ones; they look a bit like dinosaurs—anyway, there were tons of them. In autumn the leaves from the big oak tree covered the lawn, turning it gold like a gigantic leafy robot. In winter it was winter.

No one in town could understand how Mr. Gum's garden could be so pretty, greeny, flowery, and gardeny when his house was such a filthy dump.

"Maybe he just likes gardening," said

Jonathan Ripples, the fattest man in town.

"Perhaps he's trying to win a garden contest," said a little girl named Peter.

"I reckon he just quite likes gardening," said Martin Launderette, who ran the launderette.

"Oy, that was my idea!" said Jonathan Ripples.

"No, it wasn't," said Martin Launderette.

"You can't prove it, fatso."

In fact they were all wrong. The real reason was this:

Mr. Gum had to keep the garden tidy because otherwise an angry fairy would appear in his bathtub and start whacking him with a frying pan. (You see, there is always a simple explanation for things.) Mr. Gum hated the fairy, but he couldn't work out how to get rid of it, so his only choice was to do the gardening or it was pan-whacks.

And so life went on in the peaceful town of Lamonic Bibber. Everyone got on with his or her business, and Mr. Gum snoozed the days away in his dirty house and did lots of gardening he didn't want to do. And nothing much ever happened, and the sun went down over the mountains.

(Sorry, I nearly forgot. Something did happen once, that's what this story's about. I do apologize. Right, what was it?

Um . . .

Oh, of course! How could I be so stupid? It was that massive whopper of a dog. How on earth could I forget about him? Right, then.)

One day a massive whopper of a dog—

(Actually, I think we'd better have a new chapter. Sorry about all this, everyone.)

2
A Massive Whopper of a Dog

One day a massive whopper of a dog came to live on the outskirts of town.

Where did he come from? Nobody knows. What strange things had he seen? Nobody knows. What was his name? Everybody knows. It was Jake the dog. He was a furry wobbler and friendly as toast, and he soon made himself very popular. He would often come into town to play with the children and give them rides on his enormous broad back. No matter how many children wanted a ride on him, he never grew tired. He was just that sort of dog. If he had been a person, he probably would have been a king, or at the very least a racing car driver with a cool helmet.

Or perhaps he would have been a gardener, because Jake the dog loved nothing

more than playing in gardens. He enjoyed rolling his big doggy body around on a springy green lawn to see what it felt like (generally it felt like a lawn) and chomping up the flowers in his big doggy mouth to see what they tasted like (generally they tasted like flowers). He looked so happy that nobody really minded his messy visits. In fact, a rumor began that if Jake the dog visited your garden, it meant you were in for some good luck, and if he left a "little gift" on the lawn, you were in for double good luck, and maybe even a telegram from the queen.

So the townsfolk started to leave pies and bones out on their lawns, hoping to tempt Jake into their gardens. Sometimes it worked and sometimes not. Mostly he played where he liked and when he liked. He was a free spirit, like Robin Hood or the Man in the Moon or something, I dunno—he was just a dog, after all. All summer long Jake played, and everything was fine until the fateful day he discovered a garden he'd never played in before. It was the prettiest, greeniest, floweriest, gardeniest garden in the whole of Lamonic Bibber.

On that fateful day Mr. Gum was snoozing away in his unmade bed. (I told you he was a lazer, and that's what lazers do.)

He was dreaming his favorite dream, the one where he was a giant, terrorizing the townsfolk. His enormous bloodshot eyes flashed evilly like flying saucers high up in the clouds as he snatched the roofs off houses to steal the toys from the children's bedrooms. Nobody could stop him. He was the biggest and the best, he was—
WHACK!!

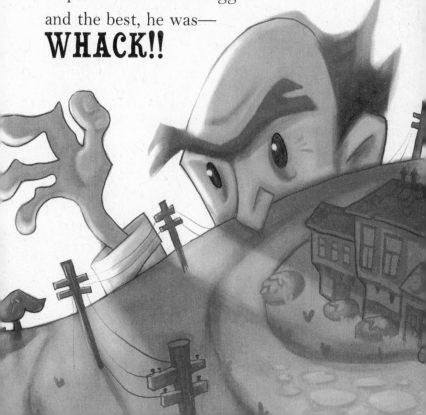

For a moment Mr. Gum did not know what was happening. Where were the tiny houses? Where were the frightened people? Where were the— **WHACK!!!**

"Ow!" yelled Mr. Gum, rubbing his head and looking around in terror. "Oh, no!" he rasped. The angry fairy was hovering over him, frying pan at the ready.

"Sort out the garden, you lazy snorer!" yelled the fairy, and down came

the frying pan. Mr. Gum was too fast this time and shot out of bed like a guilty onion. **PFFF!** went the frying pan as it hit the bedcovers, sending up a little cloud of dust and ants.

Mr. Gum legged it out of the bedroom and went hurtling down the stairs. He stepped on an old slice of pizza lying in the hall and skidded into the kitchen, riding it like a cheese-and-tomato surfboard. He could hear the fairy right behind him, shrieking with fury.

"I 'aven't done nothin' wrong! I kept the flippin' garden TIDY!" shouted Mr. Gum as he flung open the back door and ran outside. He started to say something else, but when he saw the garden, the words got stuck in his throat. They tasted horrible.

The garden was not tidy. The garden was a total wreck. The lawn was tufted up and torn. The flower beds were trampled and chewed. Rose petals and sunflower heads lay scattered all over the place like rose petals and sunflower heads. There was something lying under the oak tree that Mr. Gum did not even want to think about. And in the center of the wreckage played the most monstrous dog Mr. Gum had ever seen.

It was Jake, of course. The beast was rolling around for his own fun, his golden brown

fur matted with
grass, his happy eyes squint-
ing into the sunshine.

Before Mr. Gum's disbelieving eyes,

nine moles popped out of their holes and joined the party. The two smallest ones began bouncing up and down on Jake's furry belly and doing somersaults. The rest of them chased one another in circles or had races.

WHACK!! The pan came down on Mr. Gum's head faster than Super-man. **SLAP!!** The pan whipped him one on the bottom. **BOING!!** A fat one to the belly.

Mr. Gum doubled up in pain and tripled up in fear as the fairy raged. "It ain't my fault!" he yelled.

"I ain't never seen that dog before!"

"I don't care whose" **BASH!** "fault it is! It's your" **SPLURK!!** "job to" **WALLOP!!** "do the gardening" **VROINNNK!!** "you stupid trouser-face!"

Mr. Gum flung himself down on the lawn and lay there whimpering, his eyes shut tight in unbraveness. Jake, on the other hand, was having a brilliant time.

But just then a cloud shaped a bit like a bone drifted by. With a hungry bark, Jake ran off to chase it. Mr. Gum watched as the dog bounced over the

fence and disappeared off to who knows where. The moles raced back to their mole holes at the speed of moles. As suddenly as it had begun, the terror was over.

Mr. Gum spent all afternoon repairing the damage. The fairy watched him, scowling and brandishing the frying pan dangerously to hurry him on. Eventually the garden was back to normal, and with one last **WHACK** for good

measure, the fairy flew back to the bath-tub and vanished. Mr. Gum breathed a sigh of relief and went inside to find he'd missed his favorite TV show, *Bag of Sticks*, which was a broadcast of a bag of sticks for half an hour. (Mr. Gum was the only person in the country who ever watched *Bag of Sticks*. Everyone else tuned in to watch *Funtime with Crispy*.) "That dog ought to be given a meddling medal, he's such a meddler," muttered Mr. Gum. "I hope that's the last of him."

But it wasn't the last of Jake, it was the beginning. Jake's big doggy brain could not stop thinking about that amazing garden, and the very next day he returned with much the same result as before. And the day after that. And the day after that. But not the day after that, because it was Wednesday and everyone knows that

dogs have the day off on Wednesdays.

But on Thursday you should have seen him! He was back with a vengeance. Every day (apart from Wednesdays) it was the same story. That massive whopper of a dog would come bouncing over the fence and start romping around like an uncontrollable doctor, sometimes leaving his "little gifts," as was only natural. Mr. Gum would run out into the garden shaking a fist on the end of a stick to frighten him off, but he could never catch him. Jake would just bark like a cheeky schoolboy doing an impression of a dog barking. Then he'd bounce over the spiky fence and disappear off to who knows where.

Three weeks later Mr. Gum was covered in frying pan–shaped bruises and he had missed ten episodes of *Bag of Sticks*. It was time for action. Nasty action.

"It's time for action," said Mr. Gum to nobody in particular. "Nasty action."

Nobody in particular shrugged his shoulders and wandered off to eat his dinner. Mr. Gum went to the shed and got out his thinking cap. He put it on his knee (it was a kneecap) and started thinking about how to get rid of that dog.

3

Mr. Gum Lays His Plans Like the Horror He Is

The next morning Mr. Gum was in the butcher's shop. The butcher was a scrawny old man named Billy William the Third, and no one knew what the "the Third" bit meant.

"I reckon he was in prison when he was younger and his number was Three," said Jonathan Ripples, the fattest man in town.

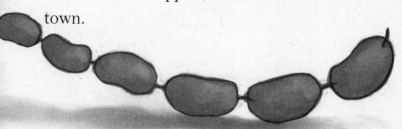

"Maybe it's because he's the Third Nastiest Person in town," said the little girl named Peter.

"Tell you what I think," said Martin Launderette, who ran the launderette. "When he was a young man, he was probably in prison and—"

"HEY!" said Jonathan Ripples. "Stop stealing my ideas!"

"Shut up," said Martin Launderette. "Why don't you go on a diet?"

Of course, Billy William the Third had his own theory.

"It's cos I'm actually royalty," he would tell anyone foolish enough to listen. "I'm third in line for the throne of Engerland after them other geezers." (He always pronounced "England" in this way. Other words he said funny were "hospital," "fountain," and "funny.") Nobody believed Billy William the Third's story about being roy-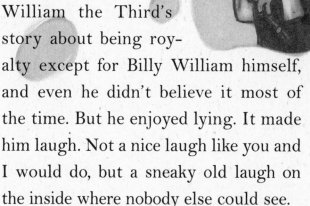alty except for Billy William himself, and even he didn't believe it most of the time. But he enjoyed lying. It made him laugh. Not a nice laugh like you and I would do, but a sneaky old laugh on the inside where nobody else could see.

Anyway, forget it, the important thing is that Mr. Gum had gone to old BW III's butcher shop (which was called Billy William the Third's Right Royal Meats) to buy the biggest load of meat he could get his angry hands on. He had a plan.

"I've got a plan," he told Billy William. "Next time that whopper dog comes a-playin' on my lawn, well, he'd better watch out, that's all! My plan is the best!"

"Are you gonna be layin' down all that meat and poisoning it, so when that barking fatty eats it, he'll fall down dead?" guessed Billy William.

"Maybe I am," said Mr. Gum, a little annoyed that the butcher had guessed his plan so quickly. He had been looking forward to explaining it in detail and impressing Billy William with his cleverness and bad heart.

"Talking of bad heart," said the butcher, "here's three pounds of it. It's been sitting out in the sun since last Tuesday. That ought to poison him and no mistake, Mr. Gum me old slipper!"

"Why did you leave it sitting out in the sun?" said Mr. Gum, taking the horrible sloppy bag from the disgusting butcher.

"I like watching the flies go mad over it!" Billy William laughed. "They're funty!" (You see, that was how he pronounced the word "funny.") "It's the funtyiest sight in all of Engerland! I laughed so hard, I nearly had to go to the hoppital!"

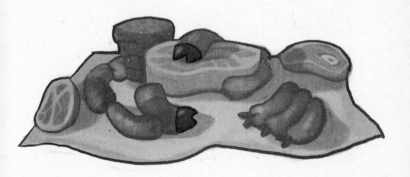

"Well, thank you, me old gobbler," said Mr. Gum, handing over some money that Billy William would later discover to be made out of lies and broken promises. And with that, Mr. Gum left the shop.

Out in the high street he remembered he hadn't been nasty to anyone in more than ten minutes. He looked around for any children who might be playing or just walking or anything—it didn't really matter what they were doing, even reading a book would be fine. Just some children he could be nasty to. But there were none to be seen, so he went and bought a newspaper. He opened it up at a photo of a ten-year-old boy who'd just won the World Record Cup Reward for Secret Burping.

"This'll do nicely," said Mr. Gum,

and he scowled at the photograph all the way home, hardly even looking where he was going. At one point he tripped over a stone, which made him feel like the Burper was somehow beating him, but that only made him scowl harder than ever. "So you see, I've won again," he said with a proud smile that he quickly turned back into a scowl.

Sunny, unseasonably cool. High 6 C/

Metro Edition

Secret Burping Champion Crowned
10-year-old: I'm burping right now

By Jim Rivera, 12

From the back room of a photo lab at Stone and Spadina, a human rights campaign is developing that's attracting worldwide exposure.

Between customers, Toronto's Yogesh Varhade retreats into his tiny office where bookshelves groan under the weight of documents and research material.

The 40-year-old Indian-born man donates all his spare time during his current stint at his handbook.

For almost 30 years, he has been fighting the worst of the caste people from untouchables on the last few years it.

But if only in the last few years it.

Up Front

Racial Discrimination when an argued the caste system is a cruel and oppressive form of ethnic oppression.

The committee's last asked India to report back in January 1996, on the progress it has made to eradicate a law for their Scheduled Caste and to ensure constitutional.

Back home Mr. Gum locked all the doors and windows, even the broken ones. Then he sat down to think on the old sailor's chest that stood in the front hall. It was a beautiful old thing made of mahogany, which is a type of wood called mahogany, and it was carved all over with amazing scenes of life at sea with waves and whales and tall ships. Mr. Gum had

owned the sailor's chest for more than forty years, but he had never once taken the time to appreciate its beauty.

What's more, Mr. Gum had never once thought to open that beautiful chest and see what was inside. Had he done so, this might have been a very different story indeed. This might have been *Mr. Gum's Chocolaty Adventure*, because I'll tell you something. That old chest had once belonged to a sailor named Nathaniel Surname, the hero of the high seas. One Tuesday long ago he had saved a Spanish village from being destroyed by a terrible pirate called Kevin. As a prize, the village presented Nathaniel with the chest, which was stuffed absolutely full of chocolate. Not just any old chocolate, mind you, but special chocolate made by the dolphins of the region. And it might just be legend, but some said it was magic chocolate with fantastic powers, and they always whispered when they said it, which is why it is written so small. How the chest ended up in Mr. Gum's house nobody knows. But there it had stood for more than forty years, unloved and unopened. As a result, Mr. Gum had never discovered Nathaniel's sugary treasure, which just goes to prove that angry people always miss out on their rewards. They are so busy sniping and griping that they never see the good things around them.

As the famous song says:

You've got to have eyes

Eyes for the lovely things
    in life!

If you've only got eyes

For the horrid and the bad

How you gonna get

I said how you gonna get

I said how you gonna get

The chocolate you deserve?

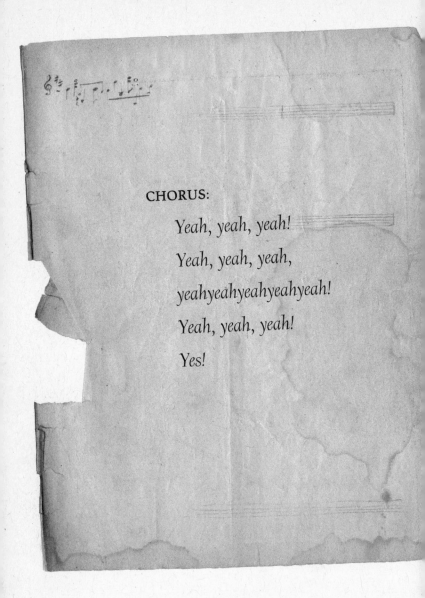

CHORUS:

Yeah, yeah, yeah!

Yeah, yeah, yeah,

yeahyeahyeahyeahyeah!

Yeah, yeah, yeah!

Yes!

You've got to have eyes

Eyes for the amazing joy and stuff!

If you've only got eyes

For old walnuts filled with spit

How you gonna get

I said how you gonna get

Tell me HOW you gonna get

The chocolate you deserve?

(CHORUS)
(GUITAR SOLO)
(REPEAT CHORUS WITH OSTRICH NOISES TO FADE)

So it was that Mr. Gum found himself sitting on a sailor's fortune of what may have been magic chocolate, in terrible ignorance, hatching evil.

"How do I know these cow hearts are gonna be rotten enough?" he asked himself presently. "I'd better try eating one myself. If it kills me then I'll know it's rotten enough to use on that big woofer."

He took out a cow heart and opened his mouth wide.

"This is one of the craftiest things I've ever done," he chuckled, raising the smelly greenish red meat to his lips. "I am a very clever man."

Mr. Gum was just about to take a bite when he realized that this might not be such a clever idea after all. He put the heart back into the bag and thoughtfully scratched his beard, not the beard that grew on his chin but a spare one that grew on the wall that he used for scratching at from time to time.

In the end he decided to soak the rotten hearts in rat poison just to be sure. "It can't fail!" he cackled. "Old dogger is in for a surprise he won't like at all!"

4
Mr. Gum Has a Cup of Tea

Mr. Gum had a cup of tea.

5

Jammy Grammy Lammy

F'Huppa F'Huppa Berlin Stereo

Eo Eo Lebb C'Yepp Nermonica

Le Straypek De Grespin

De Crespin De Spespin

De Vespin De Whoop

De Loop De Brunkle

Merry Christmas Lenoir

The next morning Mr. Gum inspected the cow hearts. They had been soaking all night in rat poison, and they were good and proper dangerous to dogs now and gave off a foul smell even worse than before.

"That blibberin' dog'll be smelling this bad smell, and with the animal instincts of animals, he'll refuse to eat 'em!" thought the crafty old man. "I'd better disguise the smell with something nice."

Mr. Gum looked through his kitchen cupboards, but was there anything nice in there? 'Course there wasn't. All he could find was a rotted turnip, a dried-up mushroom, and a sock full of stale potato chips. So off he headed into town. He was in a filthy mood, and as he walked along, he muttered to himself:

"**SHABBA ME WHISKERS**," he muttered. "Who'd've thought poisoning that stupid whopper dog could be such hard work? What a bother it all is." There was a little girl playing in the hedge as Mr. Gum walked by, and she heard what he said and grew alarmed.

"What's old Mr. Gum up to now with talk of poisoning whopper dogs?" said the little girl to herself. "What whopper dog can he mean?" She ran through a list of all the whopper dogs that she knew. It didn't take long, because she only knew one—Jake, that big lovable golden old hound.

"No!" she cried. "No! I won't let it happen! I loves that dog, watch out cos it's true! I loves him and what's more, that dog saved my life once, and now I'm not gonna stand by playing in a hedge while that old grizzler flippin' poisons him to death and destruction! No way, says I! I'll stop him, that's what I'll do!"

Now this little girl's name was Jammy Grammy Lammy F'Huppa F'Huppa Berlin Stereo Eo Eo Lebb C'Yepp Nermonica Le Straypek De Grespin De Crespin De Spespin De Vespin De Whoop De Loop De Brunkle Merry Christmas Lenoir, but her friends just called her Polly.

You will have to make up your mind now whether or not you are her friend. If you are, then you can call her Polly too. But if you are not, then every time you see the name "Polly" in this story, in your head you will have to say "Jammy Grammy Lammy F'Huppa F'Huppa Berlin Stereo Eo Eo Lebb C'Yepp Nermonica Le Straypek De Grespin De Crespin De Spespin De Vespin De Whoop De Loop De Brunkle Merry Christmas

Lenoir" instead. For instance, she's about to go running down a hill, like this:

Polly went racing down the hill like a runaway marble.

Now if you're her friend, then don't worry about it. But if you're not her friend, you will have to read it like this:

Jammy Grammy Lammy F'Huppa F'Huppa Berlin Stereo Eo Eo Lebb C'Yepp Nermonica Le Straypek De Grespin De Crespin De Spespin De Vespin De Whoop De Loop De Brunkle Merry Christmas Lenoir went racing down the hill like a runaway marble.

Most people in Lamonic Bibber chose to be Polly's friend for the sake of time and convenience. Luckily though, Polly was a girl worth liking. She was nine years old, with lovely sandy hair like a cat's daydream and a smile as happy as the Bank of England. And when she laughed, the sunlight went splashing off her pretty teeth like diamonds in search of adventure.

So Polly went racing down the hill like a runaway marble, determined to find Jake the dog before he fell victim to Mr. Gum's evil scheme. She didn't know exactly what the old man had in mind, but she knew her big friend was in trouble. She ran past the Olde Curiosity

Shoppe and then ran back because she was curious to see what was inside. Then she remembered the danger Jake was in and continued on her way. She ran past a dustbin filled with rubbish and then another one filled with rub-bish and then another one filled with rubbish and then another one filled with princesses. "Hmm, there was something unusual about one of those dustbins," she had time to think, but she had to keep on running. She ran past big trees, little trees, tiny little trees, and tiny tiny little trees so small they were more like pebbles, in fact they were peb-bles. She ran past a cat's ears that were lying on the pavement and a cat's nose and whiskers that were lying on the pavement and a cat's body and tail and legs and eyes and claws that were lying on the paveme—in fact it was all just one cat, lying on the pavement. She ran like the wind and then got tired and just walked like a breeze. But she soon sped up again, because she was determined to save that tremendous dog.

It was only after she'd been running for about half an hour that she remembered something quite important: she had absolutely no idea where Jake lived. And what's more, she was no longer in Lamonic Bibber. She had come to the woods on the edge of town, and they were big and scary and full of shadows. The ancient trees looked down from on high, stern and forbidding. "We are the trees," they seemed to whisper. "You are not welcome in this place. We are the trees." A cold wind blew, making Polly shiver, and she was certain that one of the flowers was snarling at her.

"Oh, no!" she cried, sitting down on one of those massive toadstools you sometimes get in spooky woods. "I dunno where I am, an' that old Jake's facing the

biggest challenge of his doggy life an' I doesn't know wheres to find him an' that flower's probbly gonna eat me!" And with that she burst into tears.

Just then an old man peered out the window of a secret cottage half hidden in the bushes behind her. Polly hadn't noticed the cottage, and I'm sure you wouldn't have either. That's the thing about secret cottages—they're secret.

"Well, well, well," said the old man. "What have we here? A little girl in trouble."

And here this chapter ends, leaving you to wonder if the old man was Mr. Gum or if he was a different old man who was going to be nasty to Polly and laugh at her and stuff. Or maybe he was a good man. Yes, this chapter ends here with me not telling you that Polly was sitting outside the cottage of Friday O'Leary, a fantastic old fellow who knew the mysteries of time and space and things of that nature. And with me not telling you that he is one of the heroes of this tale. Ha, ha, I am keeping that information to myself, and you will have to wait till Chapter 7 to find it out. That is what is known as suspense.

6

Mr. Gum Lays Down His Hearts

Meanwhile, Mr. Gum was a-mumblin' and a-grumblin' his way into town. He made his way past Billy William the Third's Right Royal Meats, and while he was tempted to go in, he knew that it would be a waste of time. He would never find anything nice-smelling in Billy William's butcher's shop. That was one of the reasons Mr. Gum liked him. Because he was a stinker.

There were no customers with Billy

William at that hour and Mr. Gum could see him through the dirty window. He was playing a game of Butcher's Darts, which is exactly the same as normal darts except that the board is a pig's head and the darts are old sheep's bones. Billy William had invented it one day when he was drunk. Mr. Gum loved Butcher's Darts, but there was no time to pop in and challenge Billy William to a match. He had more important fish to fry. Or rather, to poison. Or rather, dog, not fish. He had more important dog to poison.

So he continued on and crossed over to Mrs. Lovely's Wonderful Land of Sweets, which was a sweetshop at the other end of the road. As you might guess, Mr. Gum didn't enjoy going in there at all because it was a wonderland of sweets and good-

ness, and Mr. Gum was a filthy old devil who hated good things like sweets and birthday parties and kittens dressed as clowns. He would much rather hear a piano being demolished by illegal bull-dozers than a Mozart concerto. He didn't even like pop music, not even the Beatles. The only thing he liked about the Beatles was their name,

 because they sounded like insects and you could scare people with insects.

So he stepped into the sweetshop as cautiously as a paper hat in a storm. Immediately the air was full of marvelous scents. The powdery smell of sherbet lemons mingled with the odors of strawberry bombs and licorice whips. Mr. Gum felt sick. He felt as if he were being attacked by the forces of good. When he was a boy he had loved eating sweets, but that was before he turned into a bad man. Yet now he seemed to hear the voice of the boy he had once been calling to him down the years.

"Where did it go, all the good? Where, oh, where? Turn again! Turn again! You can be good again, I know it. There is still time. Turn again, Mr.

Gum!" said the voice in his head.

He looked down and saw that the voice was not in his head after all but belonged to a young boy who was standing next to him.

"Turn again, Mr. Gum! You can be good again," said the boy, offering him a fruit chew.

For some strange reason, the boy's honest face frightened Mr. Gum more than anything else in that sweetshop.

"All this talk of turning again," he snarled, shoving the boy out of the door. "I don't like it, I tell ya. It makes me feel sick!"

At that moment Mrs. Lovely came tumbling out of the back room with her kindly eyes and kindly nose and kindly ears. "How can noses and ears be kindly?" wondered Mr. Gum, but it was true. Everything about Mrs. Lovely was kindly. She was even kindly to disgraces such

as Mr. Gum, and he could not bear this. It made him want to break down inside and cry all the bad things away.

"Hello, you old witch," he sneered. "Give me some lemonade powder!"

Mrs. Lovely's eyes sparkled. "Yes, it is a beautiful day, Mr. Gum. Yes, indeed." She smiled as she measured out a bag of lemonade powder.

"I don't know what's so lovely about it, you old menace," snarled Mr. Gum, handing over some potatoes he had painted to look like coins to save money. He was annoyed to see that as soon as the potatoes touched Mrs. Lovely's hands, they turned into real money. One of them turned into a jewel with a laughing face on it.

"**SHABBA ME WHISKERS**," he growled, turning on his heel in disgust.

"A pleasure to see you as always, Mr. Gum." Mrs. Lovely beamed as the old man stormed out with the little bag of lemonade powder clutched between his elbows. "I do hope you come again soon."

Mr. Gum hardly noticed the walk home, mainly because he took a taxi. He couldn't wait to put his plan into action. Very soon he was back in his smelly kitchen. He rubbed his hands together gleefully and danced a cruel jig like a spiteful imp who'd snotted over all the presents on

Christmas morning. He opened the little bag and sprinkled its contents over the plate of rotten and poisoned cow hearts. Then he gave them a quick sniff. "**JIBBERS!**" he gasped, clutching his throat. "They smell of lemons and sunshine and friendship—I can hardly breathe!"

Holding it at arm's length, Mr. Gum took the plate of doom out into his very neat and tidy garden. He placed it right in the middle of the lawn, where Jake was sure to see it.

The day was very still. Not a single blade of grass was moving. Somewhere in the distance a chicken barked. Mr. Gum settled back in his favorite broken chair and waited to see what would happen.

7
Friday O'Leary

So now we head back to Polly, who is just where we left her, having a good old cry outside the secret cottage. Who, though, is that old man watching her from the window? You've

probably been going crazy from all the suspense, haven't you? Well, you can breathe a sigh of relief because it is none other than Friday O'Leary, who is one of the heroes of this story. The next time somebody says to you, "I hate old men. All old men are unpleasant and wicked," don't be too quick to agree with them. Take a minute to think about this tale.

"All old men are unpleasant and wicked? That's nonsense," you will say.

"No, it's not," says this somebody, whose name is Anthony. "Mr. Gum's an old man, and he's a dreadful old shocker!"

"That's true, Anthony," you say.

"And what about Billy William the Third?" says Anthony smugly. "He's as horrible as Brussels sprouts!"

"Well, you've got me there," you say. "But Anthony, you are forgetting about Friday O'Leary. He's an old man too, and he's an absolute winner!"

"Oh, I am so stupid! I forgot about Friday O'Leary!" says Anthony. "I am going away now to pay two hundred dollars to see a glass of water balanced on a horse's back, that is how stupid I am."

And you will never be bothered by the likes of Anthony again.

Just who was this O'Leary character

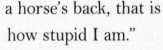

anyway? Not a lot was known about him, because he was a mysterious sort of a fellow. But I will tell you what I know based on rumors, half truths, and downright fibs.

Friday O'Leary was as old as the hills and as wise as the hills but not quite as tall as the hills. His bald head was covered in thick, curly hair, and he had the normal number of legs. He was the only person ever to have found a needle in a haystack, although to be fair it was a very large needle and a tiny haystack.

His favorite number was green, and his favorite color was twenty-six. He sometimes got his numbers and colors mixed up, and he owned the world's smallest collection of stamps (none at all). Oh, and one last thing. Occasionally, for reasons known only to himself, Friday O'Leary shouted . . .

THE TRUTH IS A LEMON MERINGUE!

. . . at the end of his sentences.

*　*　*

Anyway, earlier that day Friday had been sitting in his front room, playing the piano. He was playing a song he had written himself called "He Was Playing a Song He Had Written Himself," all about how he was playing a song he had written himself. (He had also written a song called "But He Wasn't Playing That at the Moment," but he wasn't playing that at the moment.)

He had just come to the final lines when the telephone rang. Friday ran to get it, but he was too late because it wasn't ringing in his cottage, it was ringing in Ethel Frumpton's house a hundred miles away. It was her friend Mavis on the line.

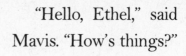

"Hello, Ethel," said Mavis. "How's things?"

Back at the secret cottage there came the sound of crying and sobbing and general unhappy little girl noises. Friday rushed to the window and uttered those famous, suspense-filled words I mentioned before:

"Well, well, well," he said. "What have we here? A little girl in trouble."

Then he opened the front door and stepped outside.

"Hello," he said to Polly. "Are you all right? **THE TRUTH IS A LEMON MERINGUE!**"

"Who are you?" asked Polly. She was a little bit nervous, because her mother had told her never to talk to strangers. Her mother was full of this sort of advice: *Brush your teeth twice a day*; *Wash your hands before meals*; *Don't cut your legs off with a bread knife*. But most of all it was *Never talk to strangers*, which was blummin' good advice, especially with a stranger as strange as the stranger before her now.

"They call me Mungo Bubbles," said the stranger, "but I don't know why, because my name is Friday O'Leary." And then Polly knew it was all right, because her mother had told her all about this remarkable man one stormy night. This is what her mother had said:

"Friday O'Leary is a mysterious old

man who lives in a secret cottage near the woods. No one knows exactly where it is, not even the prime minister. But if you are in dire need, you may find yourself there, and he will help you with your problems. Friday O'Leary, I mean, not the prime minister."

Then Polly had a thought. What if it wasn't really Friday O'Leary? What if it was a bad man pretending to be him? She remembered something else her mother had told her: "Friday O'Leary can juggle five Ping-Pong balls and a banana, and he hardly ever drops them."

So Polly asked the old man if he would

mind juggling five Ping-Pong balls and a banana for her. (Luckily she had five Ping-Pong balls and a banana in her skirt pocket.) So Friday juggled them and he hardly ever dropped them, and then Polly was convinced. Suddenly the woods looked friendly and welcoming, and Polly saw how beautiful all the nature was and how she probably wasn't going to be eaten by a flower or anything. "Friday O'Leary!" she cried. "I'm well glad to meet you! My name is Jammy Grammy Lammy F'Huppa F'—"

"I think I'll just call you Polly," said Friday.

8

Some Things Happen

Now I'll tell you what. Friday O'Leary wasn't the only character in this story with a mysterious house. Nobody knew where Jake the dog lived neither.

"I bet he lives on a farm and plays with all the other animals," said Jonathan Ripples, the fattest man in town, rubbing his chins.

"Maybe he lives in the house of a rich man who feeds him bones made of gold," said the little girl named Peter.

"This is just a guess," said Martin Launderette. "But perhaps he lives on a farm, where he plays with all the other ani—"

Suddenly Jonathan Ripples pounced on Martin Launderette and sat on him until Martin was wheezing for breath like a broken accordion.

"That'll teach you not to steal people's ideas, you skinny rubbisher," said Jonathan Ripples. "Come on, Peter. Let's go for an ice cream."

In any case, Jake didn't live on a farm and he didn't live in a rich man's house. Nobody knew where he lived except me, and I'm not telling you. Okay—I'll tell you for a dollar. Okay, fifty cents. Okay, ten cents. Come on! Ten cents! It's not much! Oh, go on! Oh, okay, you win. I'll tell you anyway.

He lived in the woods up a horse chestnut tree. He had built a great big nest up there and filled it full of old leaves that kept him warm at night. Someone had left an old radio lying around the woods, and Jake had found it one day and taken it up to his nest even though it didn't work. He was just a dog, after all.

* * *

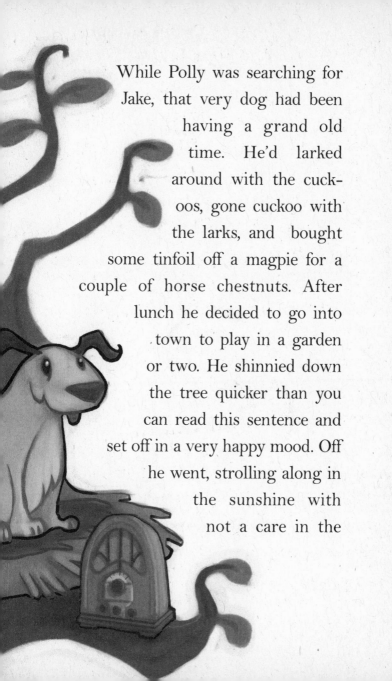

While Polly was searching for Jake, that very dog had been having a grand old time. He'd larked around with the cuck- oos, gone cuckoo with the larks, and bought some tinfoil off a magpie for a couple of horse chestnuts. After lunch he decided to go into town to play in a garden or two. He shinnied down the tree quicker than you can read this sentence and set off in a very happy mood. Off he went, strolling along in the sunshine with not a care in the world, barking and burping away and singing a song that went like this:

**BARK BARK BARK
BARK
BAAAAAAAAAAARK
BARK BARK BARK BARK
BARK BARK
WOOF**

Soon Jake came to the town. He passed Old Granny's garden with its lovely soft lawn and pond full of friendly ducks. He passed the celebrated garden of the retired wrestler Marvelous Marvin, with its rock garden in the shape of wrestling. He passed Beany McLeany's garden, where everything rhymed and the flowers grew like towers. But there was only one garden Jake fancied romping in today, and that was Mr. Gum's.

On he went on his great furry legs. Soon he came to the high street. Watching secretly from behind his greasy window, Billy William laughed to think of the nasty surprise that awaited the unsuspecting hound. "It's funty!" He chuckled to himself as Jake walked down the road and out of sight.

At last Jake came to the spiky fence that surrounded Mr. Gum's dirty house. It might have kept other dogs out. But Jake was one of those magnificent beasts that know not fear nor hesitation nor how to scramble eggs properly. He did sort of a bouncing run, and in no time at all he was over it. Well, obviously not in no time at all, of course it took some time.

But not much. He landed in the garden in a shower of dirt and flowers, and barked his welcoming bark to let all his garden friends know he had arrived. His welcoming bark went like this:

BARK!

As opposed to his normal bark, which went like this:

BARK!

The animals all recognized Jake's welcoming bark because it was so different from his normal one. Immediately the moles popped up out of their mole holes, the squirrels popped out of their squirrel holes, and the cats popped up out of their cat holes. In Mr. Gum's kitchen the toast

popped up out of the
toaster but Mr. Gum
saw it trying to
escape and scoffed it
up greedily.

"What's going on?" He
scowled—but then his eyes lit up
horridly. "I bet it's him!" he exclaimed,
spitting toast everywhere. "I bet it's that
fleabag dog!"

Very carefully Mr. Gum tiptoed over
to the kitchen window and did secret
spying with his unfriendly eyes. Outside,
Jake was racing excitedly around the

lawn, chasing his own tail. The caterpillars were so happy to see him that they
immediately metamorphosed into butterflies.

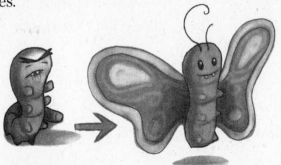

One of the caterpillars was so happy that
it metamorphosed into a donkey. The
moles squeaked, and the butterflies
roared with pleasure. The birds came

swooping out of the trees chirping like good 'uns, and the sun seemed to do magic tricks in the sky. Mr. Gum watched the whole scene unfold from behind the curtains, hating all the joy that the world was having.

"Come on, you meddler," he said under his bad breath. "Come on and eat them hearts."

Then it happened. Jake suddenly stopped barking. His nose twitched as he sniffed the scent of lemonade powder. Of course, the townsfolk were always putting out delicious treats for Jake, so he thought his luck was in. He bounded over to the plate of cow hearts in the middle of the lawn.

The other animals froze in horror as the big dog opened his mouth.

One of the moles let out a warning squeak, but he only got as far as the *squ.* It was too late. Jake's doggy jaws had already closed around a heart.

Chew, chew, chew! He chewed it up. Swallow, swallow, swallow! He swallowed it down. Go for another, go for another, go for another! He went for another heart.

But before he could take another bite, he gave a sad woof and fell over on his side, his big furry belly moving rapidly in and out. Suddenly the sun was covered up by a dirty gray cloud the size of Sweden. Behind the curtains, Mr. Gum was laughing like a robber.

9
Polly and Friday Ride into Town

Back at the cottage Polly was telling Friday O'Leary all about the danger Jake was in. Friday listened carefully, saying things like "Hmm" and "Yes, I see." Finally Polly finished her story and looked anxiously at her new friend. He was lost in thought, twirling an imaginary mustache that he thought made him look like a detective. Polly felt sure he was working on a brilliant plan.

"Tell me, Polly," he said at last. "Do

you fancy a game of tennis?"

"Tennis?" said Polly. "What about Jake?"

"Surprised exclamation! I'd forgotten all about that!" said Friday. "There's no time to lose!"

With that he disappeared into the cottage and slammed the front door shut. Five minutes later the door was flung open again and there stood Friday dressed as a tennis player.

"Here," he said, handing Polly a racket. "You can serve first because you're the guest."

"But Mr. O'Leary," said Polly as patiently as possible. "We've gots to save that big dog Jake like I told you millions of times just now."

"Oh, yeah," said Friday. "Let's go!"

He threw down his tennis racket, jumped onto his motorbike, kick-started the engine, and zoomed off like the devil himself. But a good devil, not an evil one.

"Hey!" shouted Polly. "Aren't you for-getting something?"

"Oops," said Friday, and returned to pick her up. Polly climbed into the sidecar and strapped on her helmet.

"Hold on tight! **THE TRUTH IS A LEMON MERINGUE!**" shouted Friday—and away they went.

It was a long ride into town. They passed hills and lakes and rivers and meadows and Scotland—

"Oops," said Friday. "Wrong way."

And off they belted in the opposite direction.

"Hey, Polly," shouted Friday over the noise of the engine. "What did you mean earlier when you said that Jake had once saved your life?"

"How do you know I said that?" said Polly. "There wasn't no one around when them words came out my lips."

"It's all in this book I'm reading," said

Friday, pulling a copy of *You're a Bad Man, Mr. Gum!* from his pocket. "You mentioned it in Chapter Five."

At that Polly's face grew excited and her hair grew longer.

"Maybe it says what does gonna happen to big Jake in there!" she said.

"Don't talk of what might be in the future, little miss," warned Friday. "'Tis unwise! 'Tis unwise!"

"Oh, please, please, let's look in that book!" said Polly. And she sounded so upset that Friday stopped the motorbike at once.

"Okay," he said, opening the book to the same page that you are reading right now. "But 'tis unwise! 'Tis unwise!"

No sooner had he said "'Tis unwise" than Polly read those very words on the page. As Polly read about herself reading about herself, the strangest feeling came over her. It felt like diving into a swimming pool full of rice in complete darkness, only the swimming pool was inside a mirror and the whole thing was a dream in someone's head. Well, it felt a bit like that, it's hard to describe.

With shaking hands Friday turned to the last chapter, only to find that the pages were completely blank.

"The future hasn't been written yet," said Friday, starting up the bike again. "'Tis not for us to know."

"'Twas unwise, 'twas unwise!" said Polly.

"Hey, I wanted to say that," complained Friday, revving the engine. "Don't steal my lines. Anyway, how did Jake save your life?"

"Oh, it was the usual sort of thing," said Polly as they zoomed off once more. "He rescued me from a burning centipede."

Eventually Polly and Friday O'Leary reached town. They was a-roarin' and a-bumpin' down the high street when they were spotted by Billy William the Third. Knowing how Friday was a Force for Good, Billy William jumped out from his shop and began throwing filthy old cuts of meat in their direction.

"Ha ha!" he laughed as Friday swerved to avoid a cascade of gray hamburgers. "This is just like Butcher's Darts!" He picked up a bucket of tripe and sloshed it across the road. "Take that, you Force for Good!" he shouted wildly.

"Hold tight, Polly!" yelled Friday as the bike went skidding in the slippery mess. "Tripe attack!"

Friday steered for his life, but it was no use. The wheels got all gooed up with

tripe and before you knew it he and
Polly were thrown onto the pavement.
They lay there helpless as Billy William
advanced with a sack of kidneys.

"Is this the end?" cried Friday. "Woe,
woe is me!"

But at that moment something amazing happened. A gobstopper the size of a
cannonball rolled down the street. It was
quickly followed by another one even
bigger than the first. Then another.
All of them were hurtling with deadly

accuracy toward Billy William. And they were being hurtled by none other than that wonderful seller of sweets, Mrs. Lovely.

"No!" shouted Billy William. In desperation, he threw a kidney at her but it missed by miles and landed in a tree. Mrs. Lovely didn't bat an eyelid. On she came down the high street, humming a pretty tune about a waterfall and rolling the enormous, brightly colored gobstoppers before her. Soon the street

was filled with them. Billy William hopped and dodged and swore like a footballer, but there were too many gobstoppers and down he went.

"That woman's amazing!" said Friday, his eyes shining with admiration and tripe.

"Come on, Friday! Jake needs us!" said Polly, jumping back into the sidecar. "Mrs. Lovely can sort this one out!"

Friday jumped back on the bike and hit the gas, and off they vammed down the road, the battle still raging behind them.

"I made that happen!" said Friday excitedly as they gunned along. "I mag-icked it so that Mrs. Lovely would appear at just the right moment and save us!"

Actually he had done nothing of the sort, but he wanted to keep up Polly's morale after those terrible scenes. (Also there was a tiny boastful streak in him that he couldn't help, good as he was the rest of the time.)

The two of them rode on in silence and soon they came to the high white fence that surrounded Mr. Gum's garden.

10

Jake's Darkest Hour

That fence didn't cause Polly and Friday any more trouble than it had caused Jake. They just farted over it like blackbirds.

"More meddlers!" griped Mr. Gum, dodging the angry fairy who was back with a vengeance and, of course, a frying pan. "Who needs it?"

The motorbike screeched to a halt in front of the oak tree. Polly jumped out of the sidecar and ran up to Jake, who lay on the lawn surrounded by his loyal animal friends.

The moles shook their heads sadly. A squirrel blew its nose on a butterfly. The cats looked close to tears, for Jake was the only dog they had ever loved.

Polly gasped when she saw him. The once splendid beast looked as weak as a baby. His fur had lost its shine, and his eyes were rolled toward the heavens. He was a mere shadow

of his former self, and his shadow was a mere shadow of his former self's shadow.

"Don't die on us, Jake!" she sobbed, throwing her arms around him. "You're too fat and good to die!"

Jake's only reply was a feeble little woof that sounded like a door closing.

"If it hadn't been for that butcher we could've reached him in time!" Polly sniffed.

"Time?" said Friday mysteriously. "What is time, little miss? 'Tis unwise to talk of what might have been and what might have not. 'Tis unwise!"

Polly was beginning to think that Friday was a pretty rubbish hero, but she had other things to worry about.

"What are we a-gonna do?" she wailed.

"Just you wait, and everything will turn out fine," said Friday, tapping his nose wisely. Actually, he didn't have a clue what to do, but just then Mr. Gum raced up, the fairy at his heels.

"It's no use, O'Leary!" cried Mr. Gum like the world's most evil seagull. "That dog'll never bother no one again!"

"We can still saves him!" said Polly fiercely.

"I don't think so, horrible little girl," said Mr. Gum. "Look at this."

He pointed to his own shirt, on which was written:

Champion Expert
Dog Poisoner

"That don't mean nothing," said Polly. "You just writ them words yourself in ketchup."

That shut Mr. Gum up for a minute because it was true.

"Hmm," said Friday, bending down to investigate Jake even though he was secretly a bit scared of dogs. Suddenly he stood up, his imaginary detective's mustache back in all its glory.

"Tell me, Gummy me boy," said Friday, twirling his invisible mustache cunningly. "What is the one thing that can cure that big whopper of a dog there?"

"Why, you know as well as I do, you crazy turkey!" Mr. Gum chuckled. "The only thing what can bring a dog back from the brink is the tears of a man reunited with his long-lost brother. And that's not going to happen, now, is it?"

"Hmm," said Friday grandly, wagging a finger like he imagined a detective would. "The tears of a man reunited with his long-lost brother, you say? Well, guess what, Mr. Gum? YOU are my long-lost brother, and I have a picture of us together when we were small, and when you grew older you went over to the dark side and became a bad man and forgot all about me, your brother, who is a Force for Good, and now look at what you have been reduced to: poisoning a happy bouncer of a dog just to avoid a whacking from a fairy, like the cowardly, bitter old thing you have become; and now that I tell you this amazing information, something inside you is bursting forth and you are filled with love and compassion

and dinner and you cannot help but shed tears all over this blimmin' dog and wake it up from its terrible sleep!

THE TRUTH IS A LEMON MERINGUE!"

Triumphantly, Friday handed Mr. Gum a battered photograph from the old days. It showed Friday when he was but a lad, standing next to another boy.

"That other boy is you!" said Friday. "Now bring on those tears!"

The animals gasped and Polly clapped her hands together in delight.

Mr. Gum peered closely at the photo. "Nah, that ain't me," he said. "We ain't long-lost brothers at all, you weirdo."

"Oh," said Friday. He turned to Polly

miserably, his imaginary mustache droop-
ing like an imaginary weeping willow.

"Well, little miss," he said softly, "I
did my best."

Suddenly it was all very quiet, like the
sad bit of a story. No birds sang at that
unhappy hour, no wind stirred. For once
even the angry fairy was silent. The only
sound was Jake breathing in and out,
weaker each time.

"Good-bye, Jake." Polly sniffed, bury-
ing her head in his fur. "You was a good
old boy, you was."

Just then someone tapped her on the
shoulder. She looked up to see a little boy
she had never seen before. Somehow,
though, Polly felt as if she'd known
him all her life. A feeling of great peace
and warmth spread through her, and—
"It's that nightmare from the sweetshop!"

Mr. Gum exclaimed. "How did he get here?"

"Turn again, turn again, Mr. Gum!" said the boy with his beautiful honest face.

Mr. Gum backed away, his hands raised as if to ward off a ghost.

"I don't like it one bit!" he said in a quivering voice. "Appearing out of nowhere an' talking of turning again, I don't like it!"

"I know you can be good again," said the boy, offering him another fruit chew.

That was enough for Mr. Gum. He gave a terrified yelp, clambered over the fence, and scooted off down the road, the boy's words still ringing in his ears.

The little boy turned back to Polly.

"Child," he said, even though he was no older than she. "Listen carefully. You must zip into Mr. Gum's house and look inside the sailor's chest that stands in the front hall. It is full of magic chocolate with fantastic powers," he whispered. "Do not tarry, but bring me as much as you can."

Polly didn't wait to hear any more but zipped into the house. There in the hallway stood the chest. It was the only beautiful thing in that lonely place, and it seemed to shine with hope and furniture polish. She threw open the lid, looked inside, and found nothing at all.

The chest was completely empty.

11

How It All Turned Out

It had been too long. All the chocolate had turned to dust or been eaten by sailors.

Any other girl would have given up right then and sunk to her knees in despair on Mr. Gum's yuck carpet. But Polly wasn't any other girl, she was Polly. So into the dark depths of that chest she climbed. It was much larger than it had looked from the outside and it smelled of old sea adventures and underwater business. She scrabbled around on the wooden floor, lost in the darkness, crying, hardly even remembering what she was looking for anymore. She had a horrible feeling that she was tarrying, even though she didn't really know what that word meant.

"Well, I don't care," she sobbed. "I'll tarry forever if that's what it takes to saves big Jake. And what's more—"

Just then Polly's hand closed on something small, hidden right at the very back. Slowly, her heart pumping like one of those things you use to blow up balloons, she brought it into the light. On her palm lay a single chocolate in the shape of a dolphin, the very last piece of Nathaniel Surname's treasure from that Tuesday long ago. Just once it seemed to wink at her, but it could have been a trick of the light rather than a trick of the confectionery.

"You're our last hope, chocolate," said Polly, flabbing out of the chest as fast as she could. "I just hopes you're enough to save big Jake."

"You have done well, child," said the little boy when she returned. "Now let us see if the legends are true."

Tremblingly, Polly held Jake's jaws open and tenderly stuffed the chocolate down his gob. Just as soon as it went on his tongue it turned into a real dolphin, all silvery blue, and went sliding down his throat doing whistling noises.

For a moment nothing happened. Then Jake's eyes flickered open and he uttered a little bark. It felt good, so he did another one, a little bit louder and stronger than the first. With that second bark the day was saved and the bad stuff was at an end. The angry fairy disappeared in a puff of blue smoke that smelled like bacon and eggs, and the sun came out and started doing its magic tricks again, even better ones than before with real cards this time. The moles bounced up and down with glee and the butterflies punched their little fists into the air in triumph.

Jake got up and did a victory lap around the garden to show he was back for good. Then he did a victory lick of Polly's face with his big pink doggy tongue until she was giggling like a werewolf.

"You are no ordinary lad," said Friday, turning to the boy. "Who are you really?"

"I am the Spirit of the Rainbow," answered the boy, "and it is my job to make the world glow with happy colors so that we can all live peacefully togeth—"

"Spirit!" yelled a woman's voice from next door. "Yer tea's ready!"

"Sorry, gotta go or my mum will kill me," said the Spirit of the Rainbow, and off he ran for his tea.

Well, I'll tell you what. The rest of that day was brilliant. Friday and Polly marched into town on Jake's broad back and all the animals danced capers about them and a squirrel puked up from all the excitement and everyone laughed. Friday played a flute up one nostril and a trumpet up the other, and all the good people of Lamonic Bibber came out and cheered and waved flags and ate feasts. (Jonathan Ripples ate an entire feast by himself and spent most of the next day in bed.)

On and on marched the joyful procession, getting bigger all the while and heading toward Mrs. Lovely's Wonderful Land of Sweets. But as they were crossing the town square, Mrs. Lovely herself ran up to greet the heroes. Apart from a chicken liver hanging from one arm, the courageous woman was fully recovered from the wars against Billy William the Third.

When he saw Mrs. Lovely, Friday's eyes went all shiny with admiration once again and feelings swept over him like rocket ships. He got down on one knee in the middle of the town square. Then he got down on two knees. Then he got down on three knees, which hardly anyone else in the world can do. "Mrs. Lovely," said Friday through a megaphone so everyone could hear. "You are the best. Do you fancy getting married?"

The crowd held its breath. A mole did a dramatic drumroll with a drum and a bread roll.

"All right," said Mrs. Lovely. "I wasn't doing anything this weekend anyway."

The whole town erupted with the biggest cheer yet. The butterflies rained down like confetti, and Jake did a massive happy bark as if he understood exactly what was going on. Actually, he was barking at a twig he'd just noticed, but there you go. He was only a dog, after all.

"Well, that's that then," said Friday. "Let's get in on the feasting action!"

But Polly had had a thought.

"Where's that old Mr. Gum got to?" she said.

"He's probably off getting drunk with

Billy William," guessed Friday, and he was right.

That's exactly what those two were up to, hating the world and falling over from the beer.

"But do you think he'll be back?" said Polly.

Friday looked mysterious.

"Who can say what will be, little miss?" he said.

"'Tis unwise, 'tis unwise," said Mrs. Lovely. And Friday didn't even mind that she had stolen his line, because he was crazy in love and there was marrying to be done.

And so life went on in the peaceful town of Lamonic Bibber, and everyone got on with his or her business. Friday married Mrs. Lovely, and they invited

Polly over for Sunday roasts. (And occasionally Friday did a few Sunday boasts because of that tiny boastful streak in him, good as he was the rest of the time. But no one minded.) And Mr. Gum and Billy William weren't seen for quite a while, and Martin Launderette apologized to Jonathan Ripples, and Jake the dog played happily in gardens all summer long. And nothing much ever happened, and the sun went down over the mountains.

THE
END.

I know what you're thinking. You're thinking, "How come the story's ended but there's all these extra pages at the back? I bet there's a **SECRET BONUS STORY** hidden away somewhere."

Well, forget it. The rest of these pages are just blank, empty space with nothing written on them, certainly not a **SECRET BONUS STORY**.

So just put down this book right now. It's over. Go and hassle your mum for a cookie or something.

Stop looking for a **SECRET BONUS STORY**. There isn't one, just accept it.

See? Blank, empty space. That's all.

The rest of this book is just blank, empty space.

Blank, empty space.

Blank, empty space.

The rest of this book is just blank, empty space.

Tra-la-la-la-la.

Are you still here? Look, I'm not going to tell you again. **THERE IS NO SECRET BONUS STORY. THIS IS THE END OF THE BOOK.**

THE END.
GAME
OVER.
GO HOME.
BYE BYE.

Friday O'Leary
Explains
the Universe

One day Polly and Friday were strolling down by the Lamonic River where the water rushes grow. It was one of them brilliant afternoons when the sun's shining and there's no school because it's burned down or it's Saturday or something, and there's hardly any wasps around to muck things up.

"Friday," said Polly thoughtfully. "I'm only a little girl and that, and I don't know nothin' 'bout the universe and stuff. Can you help me out with your wisdoms?"

"I'm glad you asked me that," said Friday, "because the universe is my specialist subject and I am the winner of quizzes where that's concerned. But let us sit 'neath the apple tree in the Old Meadow yonder, for that is the best place to hear my famous teachings."

So off they yondered to the Old Meadow and sat themselves down 'neath the apple tree, and there Friday began spreading his tremendous knowledge.

"A million million years ago, before your uncle was born," he began, "a tiny piece of cheese was floating in the middle of space when suddenly everything went crazy. It did a Big Bang and went flying everywhere like an

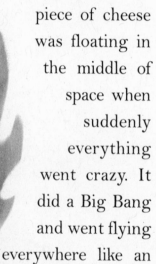

old lady at a rummage sale. For a minute or two everything smelled of cheese. Then suddenly planet Earth appeared because of scientific chemicals, and the next thing you know, a creature started grow- ing in the sea."

"What sort of a creature?" asked Polly.

"A gray one with teeth and a necklace," replied Friday, nodding wisely. "It soon got bored of just swimming around all day, so it got out of the sea, shook itself off, and started eating plants and dirt. One day, no one knows why, it turned into a woolly mammoth and got stuck in the

ice. Then cavemen appeared, Rome fell down in an earthquake, Shakespeare invented writing and football, everyone died of the plague, a bloke discovered America under a bush, and here we all are today in our modern times, walking about with computers up our noses."

"I see," said Polly. "And what about all them other planets, like Mars and Jupiter and Venice?"

But Friday's only answer was a happy snore. For spreading knowledge is a tiring business and besides, it was very comfortable 'neath the apple tree.

As Polly walked home, she thought about how lucky she was.

"'Cos some children haven't got Teachers of the Universe like Friday to do wisdoms on them," she thought. "So how they gonna learn 'bout things properly? It's a shame, that's what I says."

And as for the Teacher of the Universe himself, he spent the rest of the afternoon asleep in the meadow, and when he woke up, a horse was licking his arm.

THE END.

The One and Only Official Mr. Gum Official Glossary That Tells You What Words Mean by Explaining Them Using Other Words

GOOD EVENING.

This is Andy Stanton, the author of this book. I'm writing all the way from England, so I hope you can hear me. Now, in England we do things a bit differently from you American lot. For instance, we don't walk on the "sidewalk." Nope, we call it a "pavement." And we don't go to see a "movie," we go to see a "film." And we don't read "magazines." No, we call them "yibber-tinklers."

So the nice people at HarperCollins USA (who are publishing this book) have asked me to explain some of the strange and peculiar English words that appear in it. And I said, "Okay then, seeing as you are such nice people."

And they said, "Thanks very much, Andy. Do you want a cup of tea?"

And I said, "Yes, please, because I am English."

Then we all went home. It was quite an exciting day.

So here, without further ado, is the One and Only Official Mr. Gum Official Glossary That Tells You What Words Mean by Explaining Them Using Other Words.

A-mumblin' and a-grumblin': This is when you walk around muttering to yourself and complaining about how you hate life. Don't do it. Smile instead and eat an ice cream. You'll have a much better time, trust me.

Autumn: Fall (the season, not the thing when you trip over and hurt your knees).

Bag of Sticks: This is Mr. Gum's favorite TV program. It is RUBBISH. It is just a picture of a bag of sticks for half an hour. Nothing ever happens—it is PATHETIC. DO NOT WATCH IT. Tune in to watch *Funtime with Crispy* instead!

Bank of England: This is where they make all the money in England. They just get some green paper, draw the Queen's face on it using a special pencil most probably, and hey presto! Everyone's rich. The Bank of England is in London, by the way. It's just next to the statue of Nathaniel Surname.

Barking fatty: This is an unkind way to refer to Jake the dog. It is true that he barks, but to call him a fatty is just a bit unfair if you ask me.

Beatles: Everyone in England loves the Beatles so much. But luckily everyone in America does too, so I won't bother explaining about them. If you don't know who they are, you'll find out soon enough.

Blibberin': This is a bit rude, as in "Push off, you blibberin' stinker!" Or "I hate you, you blibberin' trouserface!"

Bloke: This is an English word meaning "guy." But it is only used for boy guys, not girl guys. As in "Look at that filthy old bloke over there! He's stealing all the fried chicken from the dustbin!"

Blummin': Same sort of thing as "blibberin'."

BOING!!: See *SPLAP!!*

Butcher's Darts: There is a game in England called "darts." Fat men in pubs play it. You have to throw little pointy things (the darts) at a round board (the dartboard) and you get different scores depending on where the darts land. "Butcher's Darts" is exactly the same except the darts are old sheep's bones, and the dartboard is a pig's head. YUCK!

Captain: This describes something or somebody that is really cool. As in, "Wow, you're great at climbing trees! You're a real captain!" Or "Mmm, that cheese salad sandwich was a complete captain!"

Crocuses: I don't know if you have these in America, but we have them here in England. They are little flowers that come out in springtime. They are quite nice if you like that sort of thing. My mum does.

Cups of tea: People in England are always drinking cups of tea. "Oh, let's have a cup of tea," they say. "That will

prove we are English and not American."
Sometimes American people try to have
cups of tea to pretend they are English,
but forget it! We can always tell you
are faking it!

Dustbin: Trash can.

Duvet: This is the thing you put on the
bed that keeps you nice and warm. It is
not a blanket. Sometimes the duvet
cover has cool pictures on it, like of
Spider-Man, or some ponies if you are a
girl. Do you call them duvets too? Maybe
you do, in which case I am sorry for
wasting your time telling you things you
already know. Here is something you
don't already know: My sister's name is
Laura. Hi, Laura! I am telling America
all about you!

Film: Movie.

Fleabag: Word used to describe a cat or dog that's not very well looked after and is all covered in fleas. I can't believe that Mr. Gum calls Jake a fleabag—it's so outrageous! Jake hasn't got ANY fleas. In fact, it's Mr. Gum who's the fleabag—he hardly ever washes!

Force for Good: This is someone or something who is on the side of all the good things in the world. For instance, Friday O'Leary is a Force for Good because he is such a brilliant hero. And sunshine is a Force for Good because it makes people feel happy and sing for hardly any reason at all. But spiders probably aren't really a Force for Good, especially if you're a fly. And Mr. Gum definitely isn't a Force for Good, he's a Force for Nastiness.

Funtime with Crispy: This is the TV program you should be watching instead of *Bag of Sticks*. I have never watched it myself, but I bet it is full of laughing clowns and hilarious things like an eel falling on a beautiful lady or something.

Furry wobbler: This describes dogs such as Jake, who are:
   a) Furry
   and
   b) Wobblers
The "furry" bit shows they are furry and the "wobbler" bit shows they are absolute whoppers.

Gob: Your mouth. As in "Shut your gob, you old stinker!"

Gobstopper: Old-fashioned English sweet. It's like a big round ball of candy and you eat it, and it stops your gob from talking cos it's so huge that there's no room left to get the words out.

Grimsters: This is a word that not even many people in England know. My friend Sandy made it up and I stole it to use in my book. Sandy is great, you would like her. I'm not kidding, she is brilliant and she likes ice-skating. Anyway, Sandy is definitely NOT "grimsters" because "grimsters" means horrible, disgusting, filthy, and nasty. Just like Mr. Gum's bedroom and nothing at all like Sandy. Her boyfriend is called Greg, by the way. Hi,

Sandy! Hi, Greg! I am telling America all about you!

Grizzler: Someone who is always grizzling at things and being generally nasty, e.g., Mr. Gum, Billy William the Third, Darth Vader.

Horse chestnut tree: Do you have these in America? We have loads of them in England. They are great big trees and in the autumn these cool big brown seeds fall off of them and they are called "conkers." And English schoolboys play a brilliant game with conkers called . . . wait for it . . . "conkers." The game of conkers starts out as fun but it usually involves quite a lot of pain and crying by the end. I don't know what the "horse" bit means, sorry.

Jibbers!: Exclamation of extreme surprise. As in "Jibbers! Someone's hidden a snake in my tennis shoe!" Or "Jibbers! That bloke's legs are made of string and he's invisible!" Or "Jibbers! If he's invisible, how could I see that his legs were made of string?"

Lamonic Bibber: This is the name of the town where Polly, Friday, Jonathan Ripples, and all the rest of the characters live. It's really nice, but unfortunately Mr. Gum and Billy William live there too and they spoil it quite a lot, the horrors.

Lazer: This describes a very lazy person, who just lazes about all day doing hardly anything. So someone who lazes is a lazer.

Launderette: This is where you go to wash your clothes. You put the money into the slot and then you chuck your clothes into the washing machine, and about six hours and twenty-five dollars later, all your clothes have shrunk and turned pink. Fantastic value!

Lemonade powder: You add water to this and you get instant lemonade. Also in England there is something called "tiger powder." You add water to it and you get instant tigers. NO LIE!

Licorice whips: Old-fashioned English sweets.

Little gifts: I don't really want to explain these, except to say that they can appear in your garden after Jake the dog has been there. They are brown, but they are not moles.

London: This is a small village in England. It is very peaceful and there is hardly any traffic on the roads. Also, things are very cheap to buy in London. I live there, by the way. If you ever come to London, you will usually find me over by the statue of Nathaniel Surname. Come and say hello! We can have a cup of tea, even though you're secretly an American!

Marble: Those little things that are made of glass or china and you roll them around or something. If you have a lot of them you can play a game called "marbles." And if you only have one, you can play a game called "marble."

Meddler: This describes someone who is always poking his nose into things. Like, say, you are trying to do a drawing and your little sister keeps saying, "That looks nothing like a tree, it is useless! It should have more branches! And you have got that car wrong, it should have loads more wheels and a ballerina should be driving it!" Well, then, she is being a meddler and you are allowed to call her a "meddling trouser-face."

Me old gobbler: Mr. Gum and Billy William are always calling each other this sort of thing. I think a "gobbler" means a "turkey," because it is always making "gobbling" noises. But I don't know for sure because I am quite stupid and I didn't really write this book. My four-year-old brother did. DON'T

TELL ANYONE OR THEY'LL SEND
ME TO JAIL!

Me old slipper: Mr. Gum and Billy
William are always calling each other
this sort of thing. A "slipper," by the
way, is one of those soft shoes that your
grandpa sometimes wears inside the
house. No one knows why, slippers are
things that just seem to appear in old
people's houses.

Moles: Oh, come on. You must know
what moles are. They are those things
that are always tunneling in your lawn,
you know. They make little molehills
and they are brown and stuff. Do I have
to explain everything?

Mum: Mom.

Nasty Action: This is when you do something that isn't very nice, such as spitting in someone's milkshake or covering your dad in live rats while he's asleep on the beach.

Nathaniel Surname: He was one of England's most famousest heroes of the high seas. He won many battles and also he held the World Record Cup Reward for Secret Burping for three years running! What a hero he was! There is a huge statue of him in London— everyone loves it and throws cups of tea all over it for good luck.

Olde Curiosity Shoppe: This is a sort of old-fashioned junk store and it is spelled all wrong because back in the Olden Days they always spelled things wrong.

In the Olde Curiosity Shoppe you can find all sorts of interesting things, like a stuffed gorilla with no head, weird old coins with pictures of soldiers on them, and an old wedding dress no one wants. And everything is covered in dust, especially the old man who works there.

One of those things you use to blow up balloons: One of those things you use to blow up balloons.

Pan-whacks: This is what you get if someone whacks you with a frying pan. I hope you never get pan-whacks, but also, I hope you never give someone else pan-whacks. The only person in the world who deserves pan-whacks is Mr. Gum. So remember: If you are thinking of giving someone pan-whacks, make sure it is Mr. Gum you are giving them to. Otherwise don't bother. Just use the pan to fry an egg instead.

Pavement: Sidewalk.

Prime minister: In England we don't have a president, we have a prime minister instead. He does the same sort of stuff as the president, except he does it in England and he drinks a lot more cups of tea while he is doing it. Also, believe it or not, we once had a prime minister who was a woman! Only she disguised herself as a bloke by wearing a suit and a false mustache. Some people liked her, but most people thought she was a bit of a wafflemonger.

Pub: Bar. This is where naughty people go to drink beer, and their faces turn red and then they are sick all over the place. But you are not allowed into pubs until you're all grown up, so don't even try it, kids, forget it!

Robin Hood: This is a guy from England in the Olden Days. He used to run around all over the place, stealing from the rich and giving to the poor. He dressed in green so he could disguise himself as a tree or a frog in case the sheriff came along. No one knows if he really existed, or whether he was just a dream or some kind of hilarious joke, but one thing's for sure—he was a total captain.

Scotland: It's a place near England where everyone's got beards, even the women. And the men wear skirts and everyone shouts a lot and has an okay time. By the way, it's freezing up there in winter, so don't bother.

Shabba me whiskers!: Mr. Gum is always saying this. It is a good example of sniping and griping. Mr. Gum is always saying things like this because he hates everything good and is constantly annoyed by life.

Sherbet lemons: Old-fashioned English sweets.

Skinny rubbisher: Someone who is thin and not very good, such as Martin Launderette.

Sniping and griping: This is when you

go around moaning and complaining about everything because you hate life. It is like a-mumblin' and a-grumblin', only a bit louder usually.

SPLAP!!: See *SPLURK!!*

SPLURK!!: See *WALLOP!!*

Stinker: Someone or something that stinks. You see, that wasn't so difficult to work out, was it?

Strawberry bombs: Yes, you guessed it—even MORE old-fashioned English sweets. Golly, isn't this glossary exciting?

Sunday roast: This is a traditional thing you eat on Sundays in England. It is

usually roast beef and Yorkshire pud-
dings (these are like great big dumplings,
mmm) and gravy and potatoes and
maybe some carrots but you can probably hide those under the table when your
mum's not looking. Or it could even be
roast lamb with mint sauce instead of
beef. But either way it's totally delicious
unless you're a vegetarian and you only
get the carrots and stuff, bad luck!

Sweets: Candy.

Tarry: No idea, sorry.

Telegram from the queen: In England,
the queen sends you a telegram if you
turn one hundred years old. It is her way
of saying, "Congratulations on being so
ancient." At least, she used to. I don't

know if she does anymore. Also, when she turns one hundred, perhaps she will have to send herself a telegram. What a strange country England is. As for the telegram itself, it's like an email from the Olden Days before they had emails. And instead of getting it on your computer, it was delivered straight to your door by a posh bloke in a uniform with silver bits on. EXCELLENT BEHAVIOR!

THE TRUTH IS A LEMON MERINGUE!: No one knows what this actually means except for Friday O'Leary. And sometimes, I think even HE doesn't really know either.

Tripe: Cow's stomach that has been boiled up and is all stringy and slimy. YUCK! Some people eat it. DOUBLE

YUCK! Some people take baths in it! Not really! But if they did—TRIPLE YUCK!

Trouserface: In England, pants are called "trousers." So this is like calling someone "pantsface!" It is not very polite, and if you call someone a trouserface you should run away fast in case they call you something horrible in return like "wafflemonger!"

Unbraveness: The opposite of braveness. If you are unbrave you will not be a hero and save the day. Instead you will simply run away and hide in a broom closet until the trouble is over.

VROINNNK!!!: See *BOING!!*

Wafflemonger: Someone who sells

waffles. Also a mean name to call someone in England. People often call the
prime minister a wafflemonger.

WALLOP!!: See *VROINNNK!!!*

Whopper: This basically means something really big. As in, "Oh my goodness!
Look at that gigantic raspberry! It's an
absolute whopper!" Or it can mean
something that is really cool, a bit like
"captain." As in, "Wow, that film was so
brilliant, it was a whopper! Especially
the bit where that eagle turned into a
robot!"

**World Record Cup Reward for Secret
Burping:** This is a championship that
takes place once every seven years in
England in a lovely little town called

Wample-Upon-Stample. You win it by doing the best secret burps, which are burps that no one else can hear and also you have to do them underwater. The judge is a moth called Emily Buttercup.

Yibber-tinkler: Magazine. As in "This is a really good yibber-tinkler, it's got brilliant pictures and stories in it. It's an absolute captain!"